He stood up, started to turn back toward the faire, then stopped. He couldn't see the water or transmission towers that he'd noticed earlier beyond the trees, but there was a church steeple. And beyond that, he could just make out a large stone building. In the harsh midday light, it looked a little like a castle.

Come off it, Kevin, he griped at himself, fighting down the sudden tightness in his stomach. Insanity must be catching. He turned back to the faire. It was gone.

No pavilions, no banners, no throngs of role players and camera-toting tourists. No parking lot for the public's cars and the participants' trailers. Nothing.

All that reached his ears was the trilling of the birds and the distant moo of a cow. . . .

ALL'S FAIRE

Pamela F. Service

FAWCETT JUNIPER • NEW YORK

RLI: $\dfrac{\text{VL 6 \& up}}{\text{IL 6 \& up}}$

A Fawcett Juniper Book
Published by Ballantine Books
Copyright © 1993 by Pamela F. Service

All rights reserved under International and Pan-American Copyright Conventions. Published in the United States by Ballantine Books, a division of Random House, Inc., New York, and simultaneously in Canada by Random House of Canada Limited, Toronto.

Library of Congress Catalog Card Number: 93-90081

ISBN 0-449-70421-1

Manufactured in the United States of America

First Edition: May 1993

For:
All the shoestring Shakespeareans of MCCT

1

Out at the Faire

Horses' hooves hammered over the turf as the black knight bore down on the targets. The black and red of his surcoat flapped against his dark armor while his face was hidden behind the slitted mask of the black plumed helmet. With one gauntleted hand he guided the horse; with the other he aimed the lance. Kevin held his breath as, one after another, the point slipped through the small brass rings. At the end of the course, the knight pulled his great black horse to a prancing halt and raised his lance triumphantly. All five of the beribboned brass rings gleamed along the shaft.

The crowd booed and hissed.

Kevin felt like cheering. This dark knight, Despard the Despicable, was without a doubt the best in the company. He wielded sword and lance with practiced skill and guided the huge horse with ease. But he was the designated villain. The buxom wench whose role was to work up the crowd before the show had instructed everyone that the knight in black and red was the bad guy and should be roundly jeered. Cheers should go to the designated hero, Vance the Valiant, whose surcoat was sky blue and whose horse was a dainty white Arabian. The others in the troupe could be cheered or booed as people wished.

Dutifully Kevin cheered as a knight in yellow took two rings and Vance the Valiant followed with three. Taking off his befeathered black hat, Kevin fanned himself. Sweat was trickling beneath his long-sleeved purple tunic, and the waistband of his black tights was itching like crazy. Medieval-style clothes were definitely not made for Indiana summers. He looked with envy at the faire goers in their shorts and T-shirts. If it weren't for wanting to see the melon contest, he'd hustle over to someplace shady.

But they were setting up that part of the program now. A knight with a flat-topped helmet stood in the center of the lists while one of the wenches placed a large honeydew melon on his head. Now the mounted knights were ready to charge. The one in brown galloped forward but couldn't get his horse close enough. Sir Vance the Valiant nicked the melon with the edge of his sword, but it only wobbled, then stayed put. Despard the Despicable sliced his gleaming sword right through the melon, splattering green pulp in a glistening arch over the grass.

Kevin started to whoop with excitement, then caught himself. Get real, Kevin, he thought as he turned away. So some playacting knight hit a melon. Big deal.

He used to love these Renaissance faires. They were the high point of his year. From the time he was small, he'd loved going with his parents to the meetings of the local Creative Anachronists. He'd really gotten into all the medieval stuff—the singing, weapons, dances, and, of course, the costumes and food. Sometimes the kids at school made fun of him, but he hadn't cared. It was something that made him different, made him special. He was proud of having parents who were as good at playing make-believe as any kid was. Besides, he guessed the kids who made fun were really just jealous.

But now things had changed. After all, he'd be going into middle school next year. And kids there would make fun for real. They'd probably call him a nerd and a major weirdo with parents who dressed up in costumes, did out-of-date dances, called themselves Lord David and Lady Barbara, and addressed their son as Squire Kevin.

Kevin wasn't sure he wanted to feel different and special anymore. In middle school he'd be in with lots of kids who had never known him before, so this was his chance to start over and fit in. Or maybe he could even get on the basketball team and be special with something *real*.

Sullenly Kevin tromped across the "faire grounds," the farm field always used for this event.

Every year he and his parents did several of these faires around the Midwest, but many of the other reenacters, like this troupe of knights and some of the Gypsies and merchants, made a part-time job of it, traveling around the country.

Kevin's short black boots squelched over turf sodden from yesterday's rain. But otherwise the day seemed perfect for bringing in the tourist money. Colorful sunlit banners snapped in the breeze against a cloudless blue sky. From brightly striped tents merchants called their wares, treasures ranging from swords and jewelry to pottery, weavings, and modern books on things medieval. Savory clouds of smoke rose above the grilled bratwurst and chicken, and though it was still morning, the tent for beer, mead, and lemonade was doing brisk business. Costumed singers warbled their madrigals, jugglers juggled, Gypsies danced, Punch and Judy performed on one stage and human actors on another. And mingling with the picture-snapping public were people who'd been recruited to dress as monks or peasants or lords and ladies and wander about keeping in character and talking to visitors as if they really were at a thirteenth-century fair.

Kevin gazed about, then pushing down a twinge of the old excitement, fixed his face into a sneer. All these adults playing dress-up and make-believe. Wouldn't they ever grow up?

Ahead was the roped-off space where his parents'

group staged their mock combat and medieval dances. He could see his mother helping his father into the padded "armor." One of the other "ladies," clutching her lute, hurried past him, calling, "Good morrow, Squire Kevin."

Kevin only grunted and changed course. No way was he going to answer, "God go with you, Lady Marcia," as if Marcia Schultz, the tax consultant, were really some fine medieval lady. If he could grow up and face the real world, why couldn't they?

He reached the spot where trees edged up to the open space and the flat field became a slope covered with tall grass and prickly wildflowers. At the bottom were more trees, but beyond them Kevin could see a water tower and power lines. If he concentrated, he could block out the faire's music, voices, and clashing armor to hear the distant rumble of traffic where a state highway sliced through southern Indiana. He smirked. The real world was out there somewhere, the world where adults acted like adults and kids went to middle school and played video games.

With rule-breaking glee, Kevin opened the cloth pouch hanging from his belt and pulled out a battery video game. He'd smuggled that in just as he'd strapped on his watch hidden well above the cuff of his purple tunic. It was his new digital watch that flashed date as well as time in neon green letters, and there was no way he was going without that.

Happily Kevin sat on the grass and began punching

buttons on the game and watching the display screen. To the sound of electronic beeping and buzzing, he sent his football players through different moves, with one team scoring a touchdown, then the other.

Suddenly a raspy old voice broke into his game. "Prithee, young man, what is that device of the devil you dally with?"

Kevin looked around to see an old man with wild gray hair and a wispy beard dressed up like some medieval hermit. He'd seen this bleary-eyed old guy mumbling to himself and hobbling around the grounds, really getting into the act. Kevin was suddenly fed up.

"Hey, come on, get real. I'm taking a video-game break, okay? I mean, this medieval act is fine for the tourists, but they're all way over there. Besides, I'd think someone as . . . as mature as you would have outgrown this make-believe by now."

"Tut-tut," the old man said, shaking his head. He seemed to straighten a little, and his bleary eyes snapped into glinting blue. "So you're in that phase, are you? Well, we can just hope you grow out of it, can't we?"

"Huh?"

"This childish scorning of imagination. Now, little ones, they take to imagination like a duck takes to water, but 'grown-up' youngsters start getting too big for themselves and thinking that imagination is child's play. Bah!" The old guy spat into the grass.

"What's worse, some of them never grow out of that," he continued, thumping his walking stick on the ground. "And a lot of silly geese they grow into, let me tell you. Shallow fools, the lot of them!"

Suddenly the supposed hermit leaned so close that his scraggly beard tickled Kevin's nose. "But the lucky ones, now, they grow out of that silliness. They catch on to how important imagination is, how you can't have a real world that's worth a darn without it. Remember that, lad. For a real grown-up, imagination is the key, the key to everything."

The old man turned and began chuckling to himself. "And remember, it was the hermit of the hills that told you so." His face faded to cloudy again, and he hobbled off, muttering to himself.

"Jeez," Kevin whispered, "that guy is majorly creepy." Tucking his video game away, he stood up and watched as the "hermit" mingled back into the crowd. Creepy like those weird prophets that medieval heroes are always running into. Kevin shook himself. Come on, this was just a batty old man really getting into things.

But suddenly being back among people seemed a good idea. Kevin straightened his shoulders. Time to wander around and look medieval. He wondered how they dealt with batty old men in the Middle Ages. Probably made a sign against the evil eye and left them strictly alone. Smart.

2

Of Knights and Gypsies

Kevin wandered back toward the jousting lists, stopping a few times for tourists to take his picture. The one thing he did want to do here was hang around the horses. And horses were part of the real world, after all, so he needn't feel guilty about it. He'd taken riding lessons once, and though he'd never gotten really good, he'd at least learned to recognize good horsemanship and good horses.

And no doubt about it, this jousting company had some really fine animals. Vance the Valiant's white Arabian was splendid-looking, if a bit skittish, but it was dwarfed beside Despard the Despicable's huge black stallion. That beast was so big and beefy, it looked more like something that pulled beer wagons. But at least that was authentic. He'd read that real knights' horses had been bred not for speed but for the strength to carry fully armored knights.

With the morning show over, the horses had been freed from their trappings and were grazing in the

corral while the "knights" lounged around their tents.
Kevin wondered what these guys did in the real world:
sell insurance, maybe, or pump gas or drive buses.
But at least *they* had an excuse for this role-playing
stuff. Faire organizers usually paid good money for
groups like this to come and thrill their visitors.

Walking around an oak that shaded the corral,
Kevin noticed the man who played Despard the Despicable talking with another costumed man by the
edge of the woods. That big fellow had certainly been
well cast as the bad knight. He was still wearing most
of his outfit, including the surcoat showing a black
boar's head on a red shield, but even without his helmet, the guy looked highly villainous. He had longish
black hair, dark eyes, a trimmed black beard, and a
craggy face that seemed constantly angry.

And now as he argued, he looked even angrier than
usual. The other man, now sneering under his mustache, was shorter, blond, and costumed like some
rich lord with a diamond clasp on his hat and a belt
of blue jewels glittering around his waist.

Suddenly Despard grabbed the man's collar.
"Promise or threaten whatever you wish, but I will
never let you have it!"

"Easy, old boy," the other gasped. "I could make
things a lot better for you, you know. In fact, life here
could be quite pleasant with the sort of wealth I could
provide."

"So you're bribing me with my own stolen wealth,

9

are you? How generous." He let the man loose as if he were dropping something dirty. "But if I cannot have her, believe me, I would never let her go to a vile rat like you." He paused a moment; then a gleam lit his dark eyes. "In fact, were you to die here, I could be sure of that, now, could I not?"

His hand grasped his sword hilt as the other man turned to run. Despard drew his sword and slashed at him but managed only to slice off a scrap of doublet and the bottom jewel dangling from his belt. With curses billowing after him, the blond man ran back toward the distant crowd.

Wow, Kevin thought, another set of lunatics. Were half the people who did this sort of thing really crazy? But maybe "Despard the Despicable versus the foppish lord" had been part of the show. If so, the audience had been one kid half-hidden behind a tree.

As Despard strode off toward the tents, Kevin walked to the spot where the two had just fought. A scrap of brocade fabric was lying in the grass, and beside it glinted the link of jeweled belt. Clearly that sword slash had been real enough.

Kneeling down, Kevin picked up the bit of belt, expecting to find blue glass in some cheap metal setting. But the "jewel" was finely cut, and the setting was smooth and heavy, an intricate mesh of vines and flowers that looked and felt like real gold. That blond fellow would probably be really miffed about losing it.

Kevin stood up and scanned the crowd, but the "lord" was out of sight. Slipping the jewel into the pouch on his belt, he walked back toward the heart of the faire. With two more days of this wretched event, he was bound to find him.

Ahead of him now, some "Gypsies" were performing. Kevin guessed they were another one of the professional groups who were paid to do their thing. They were awfully good at it. The spry little man dressed in a colorful vest and baggy pants had just finished his fire-eating act and was now juggling knives. Once he'd drawn a crowd, he packed up that act and pulled out a bulbous flute. As he began warbling a squealing tune, a woman leapt from a tent and began a wildly wiggling dance.

She wasn't wearing much besides a filmy rainbow skirt and a bra that looked and sounded as if it was made of coins. Kevin thought the way she made her bare stomach bulge in and out was kind of gross, but the men in the crowd hooted their approval.

After a minute a girl about Kevin's age wearing colorful Gypsy rags began moving among the crowd, shaking a basket for donations. She had a sullen, bored look on her dark face, and Kevin guessed that here was someone else who agreed about how stupid and childish this whole scene was. Maybe afterward he'd get a chance to talk with her, and they could pass the time slamming adults who wouldn't grow up.

When the dancer with the jingly bra had finished

11

and the crowd had dispersed, the Gypsy girl took her basket and joined the others in their tent. Lounging around, Kevin overheard some muted arguing, and then the girl came out and stalked across the faire grounds. With a shrug, Kevin followed.

She was heading, he realized, to the same spot he had fled to earlier, where field, forest, and sloping pasture met. Kevin felt a little ridiculous following her, but he really wanted to find a confederate here. He made himself walk up to where she stood looking out over the distant treetops.

"Hi," he said awkwardly. "I'm Kevin. I . . . I thought that if we both have to put up with this for the next few days, maybe I should say hello or something."

The girl pushed dark curls out of her face and stared at him as if he were a bug. Then her face flickered with a slight smile. "Hi, I'm Gina the Gypsy."

"Hey, nobody's listening. We can use our real names."

"All right," she said firmly. "I am Gina of the Romany. We do not use the term 'Gypsy.' I was born in my parents' wagon in Wiltshire, England, in the year twelve something-or-other. We never paid much attention to dates."

"Yeah, well. That's a good story. I'm supposed to be Kevin the Squire, son of Lord David and Lady Barbara, but frankly I get a little tired of all this make-believe. I mean, don't you think these people are old enough to start living in the real world?"

She didn't say a thing.

Kevin stumbled on. "I was watching you while you were passing the collection basket, and I . . . I just sort of thought you were thinking the same sort of thing."

The girl flounced her hair out of her eyes, and Kevin noticed a big purplish bruise on her cheek. "Well, I don't know about these others," she said, sitting huffily on the grass, "but *I* am not pretending anything. I am Gina of the Romany people, and I lived, lived *happily*, with my family in our wagons until about a year ago, when a black-hearted villain magicked me away to this perfectly nasty world. I took to living with a couple of pretend 'Gypsies' and traveling to events like this one in their strange metal wagon with no horses.

"And, yes," she almost shouted, "I *am* perfectly miserable, but I do not know what else to do or how to get home!"

To his surprise, Kevin saw real tears brimming in her eyes. She turned away and stared into the distance. This was really weird. Here was a kid his own age who was desperately clinging to her made-up character. Why? Was her real life so bad that even this pretend one was better?

Then he remembered the bruise on her face. Was she an abused child? Should he tell someone? There were a couple of officers from the county sheriff's department assigned to the faire. No, *he* shouldn't tell them, but maybe she should.

"Hey, if you're having a hard time at home, if someone is beating you or something, maybe you should tell the police or someone. That sort of thing's against the law, you know."

Her voice was trembling now. "I am not having a hard time at home because *I am not home*. These people are not terribly nice to me, and the man does hit me sometimes when I don't do as he says, but I don't mind much. I've known worse. And they did take me in, let me travel with them in their metal house and even watch their magic television box. But what I *do* mind is not being home. It is not right. I do not belong here, and I want more than anything to go back."

She gave way to shuddering sobs. What should he do now? Kevin thought, close to panic. Obviously there wasn't much point in trying to talk her out of her story. Maybe he should just humor her.

"Right. Sure, I can see that. It must be pretty sad, being so far from home. Eh . . . why don't you tell me about it, about your home. I've never been there, to England, I mean."

Slowly her sobbing quieted. "We moved around a lot," she began in a whispery voice, "but it was very beautiful near the village of Ashford, where we had camped when that villain magicked me away. The others must have moved on by now, though. It has been about a year."

Her lips were beginning to tremble again. Quickly Kevin asked, "So what is it like around Ashford?"

She began telling him. Softly her words built up a picture of a little thatch-roofed village clustered around the stone walls of a turreted castle. There were a carved cross in the center of town and a new stone church that was considered very well-off because it had two stained-glass windows.

But being Romany, she and her family didn't have much to do with churches. They went into villages only if someone wanted to do some horse-trading, or have their fortune told, or needed some healing. And, of course, if there was a market or faire, they'd go to barter things and pick a few purses. Gina said proudly that she was particularly good at purse snatching. But normally they stayed clear of non-Romany folk to travel and camp with their own kind.

"Then one day," she want on to say, "we camped in the woods near Ashford. Most of us went into the village for market day. My cousin Rhonda gets coins showered on her when she dances. My father repairs pots and pans, and my mother peddles baubles and tells fortunes. But what I am best at is snatching purses or anything else useful. I have a good, light touch and am as quick as lightning, but this time I guess I got too greedy."

The pride in her eyes faded to regret. "There was

15

a fancy lord in the market crowd wearing a really flashy jeweled belt. I had it off in a moment, but he felt it and was after me. In seconds he and his men were on their horses and hunting me like a deer. When they finally ran me down at the edge of the woods, their lord jumped off his horse and started shaking me like a dog does a rat. He got his jewels back, but when one of the others said they should hang me right there, he said, no, that was too much trouble for the likes of me. Instead he worked some terrible sorcery and sent me to this dreadful, horrible, unnatural place."

The girl turned her dark, angry eyes on him. "Kevin the Squire, this real world you are so fond of is like a nightmare for me. Every morning all I want is to see my own real family in my own real world. And I will never, ever be able to do that again!"

Once again she sank into wracking sobs. Kevin sat beside her, shaken. She had described that fair green land of hers so well that he could almost imagine it in his own mind. She might be crazy, but she was very thorough about it.

Awkwardly he reached over and placed an arm around her shoulders. "Hey, I'm sure you'll be able to—"

Suddenly the ground buckled under him, and Kevin felt himself flipping through the air, air thick and prickly as electrified glue. With a breath-jarring thump, he was on the ground, staring up at the blue, cloud-dotted sky.

Awesome. That was wilder than those cartoon versions of what happens at a first kiss. And all he had done was put his arm around a girl. Wouldn't catch him doing *that* again.

3

As in Days of Old

When he finally sat up, Kevin was surprised to see that Gina had not stalked off. In fact, she was lying not far from him on the grass, looking about as stunned as he felt. Then she, too, sat up and gazed around. Suddenly she leapt to her feet.

"Home! I've come home!"

Startled, Kevin looked about, then sighed with relief. This girl really was cracked. This was the same southern Indiana scene there'd been a moment ago. Well, at least there was a field sloping down to trees. Had the grass been sprinkled with yellow flowers before? Probably, and he just hadn't noticed. He hadn't noticed the trees being quite so broad and high either. But since when had he paid any attention to trees?

He stood up, started to turn back toward the faire, then stopped. He couldn't see the water or transmission towers that he'd noticed earlier beyond the trees, but there was a church steeple. And beyond that he could just make out a large stone building. In the harsh midday light, it looked a little like a castle.

Come off it, Kevin, he griped at himself, fighting down the sudden tightness in his stomach; insanity must be catching. He turned back to the faire. It was gone.

No pavilions, no banners, no throngs of role players and camera-toting tourists. No parking lot for the public's cars and the participants' trailers. Nothing.

Somehow he'd gotten very turned around, he thought desperately. He must have rolled way down the hill. But, really, all he had to do was listen for the sounds of the faire and head that way.

All that reached his ears was the trilling of birds and the distant moo of a cow.

Feeling queasy, Kevin looked back at Gina. She was standing with hands on hips and a carefree smile on her face.

"Don't head that way, goose. Let's see if we can find my family's camp."

"Sure, but I can't figure out where the faire is from here."

"As far as I know, it's back in the purgatory it deserves. But no, I mean my *real* family. They were camped in those woods."

She pointed to the dark sea of trees, then with a joyous laugh began spinning around, her long hair and fringed shawl swirling about her. "Home! After all that . . . that awfulness, finally home!"

19

Laughing again, she swayed dizzily a moment, then started trotting down the hill. Kevin stood gazing after her. She was suddenly like a totally different person. But surely that proved she was crazy, he told himself, sudden personality changes and all. Should he follow her, though, or let her go?

Fear began seeping up from the flower-dotted grass. No! There was nothing to be frightened about. They'd figure out soon enough where they were. But wherever that was, he suddenly did not want to be alone there.

"Hey, wait up!" he called, running down the hill after her.

He didn't catch up until she slowed at the shadowed fringe of the woods. The trees were tall, dark, and massive. They seemed to have shaded out most of the brambly undergrowth. Even the air that pooled beneath them had a different smell, a different feel.

Undaunted, Gina passed from sunlight to shadow, walking confidently along a well-beaten path. Looking around uneasily, Kevin followed. Dark tree trunks and thin shafts of sunlight stretched off in all directions as if they were in some enormous columned cathedral. Under the high, leafy canopy, the only sound besides their own footsteps was the calling of unseen birds and an occasional secret rustle from a bush.

At last the path opened onto a small, grassy clearing. Gina stopped and stared. "They've gone! This is where we camped. I know, because there's the dead oak.''

She rushed across the clearing to a gray, lifeless tree. Pointing to the ground, she said, ''Yes, there's been a fire here, several, in fact.'' Looking around, she added, ''And none seem very fresh. Do you suppose . . . Oh, no, do you think the same time passed here as it did there?''

Automatically Kevin pulled up his sleeve to look at his digital watch. The date and time display were blank. Fear gripped him again, but he shoved it down. The stupid thing must have broken in the tumble. ''Look, Gina, we've only been gone a few minutes. Let's get out of these gloomy woods and look for the faire.''

Ignoring him, Gina kicked a charred log. ''If it's been a year here, too, my family could be anywhere in England by now.''

Her voice was trembling, and Kevin thought she might start crying again. Suddenly he realized that if he didn't get a grip on things, he might, too. ''Hey, let's get real for a moment, okay? Once we find the others, we can get back into playing our parts again.'' He gave her arm a tug.

''And who might you be looking for, then?''

Startled, Kevin looked up. A bearded man was leaning against a tree. Wearing brown and green, he had a soft hat slouched over one eye and an archer's bow slung over a shoulder. Kevin relaxed. Clearly, in that getup, this was another medieval reenacter.

"I'm looking for my family," Gina said evenly. "We camped here some while ago."

"Well, now," the man said, stepping free of the trees. "This is a favorite spot for Gypsies, all right, but there haven't been any through for some time."

"Well, then," Kevin put in, "you can just tell us the way back to the faire."

"The faire? True, there is a faire starting in Ashford on account of the tournament, but that is a long way for you to have just strayed from."

"A tournament?" Gina said brightly. "There are sure to be Romanies there."

"As thick as flies on honey." The man nodded, then casually unslung his bow. "Now, do I get paid my toll for this news? I do not usually let travelers pass through these woods without paying a toll."

"Ha!" Kevin said. "I suppose you're playing Robin Hood. Well, you can just work that one on the tourists."

The man spat into the grass. "Robin Hood, bah! That upstart braggart hangs out in Nottinghamshire, not around here. And if you think that is where you are, then you are a good deal more lost than I guessed."

"Don't mind him," Gina said to the man while grabbing Kevin and pulling him toward another path. "The boy is just a bit lost in the head. But surely no woodsman would charge one of the Romanies for passage.''

The man gave a mock bow. "Ah, but surely this woodsman would, if the mood struck him.'' Then he laughed and slipped back into the trees. "But tempting the wrath of God by robbing one of his feeble-minded, that is one risk too many.''

Kevin yanked his arm out of Gina's grasp as they hurried along the path. "What do you mean by telling that jerk I'm crazy? The only ones crazy around here are the ones who can't live in the real world long enough to give or get directions.''

Gina spun around and glared at him. "To use one of your phrases, get real, Kevin. This *is* the real world—not yours but *mine*. For all I care, you can go wandering all over England looking for your phony faire, but I am heading for Ashford to look for my family.''

Kevin watched as she stalked down the path, and then he sheepishly followed. Maybe once they got out of these woods, he'd see the highway or something and get his bearings. He let that thought run through his head like a desperate prayer.

Once clear of the trees, they did see an intersection. But it was where their grassy track met a rutted dirt road. Clustered around the crossroads there were no gas stations or convenience grocery stores, only several shabby houses. Their plaster walls and thatched roofs did not look very southern Indianan.

Pamela F. Service

While Kevin stared, dumbfounded, Gina walked
up to a cottage. An old woman sat outside the door
deftly weaving baskets while chickens scrabbled about
her in the yard. "Old mother, can you tell me if any
Romanies have been by here of late? I . . . became
separated from my family a while ago and am searching for them."

The woman squinted up at Gina. "Gypsies,
humph. We have your type by too often as it is. At
nights I have to lock up every chicken and iron pot
as if I were some fine, wealthy lady." Then her look
softened a little. "But lost, are you? Well, there's sure
to be plenty of your folk heading to Ashford the next
few days for the tournament and all."

"And what tournament is that, old mother?" Gina
asked.

"Why, the one where Lady Elfrieda is finally to
choose her husband."

Gina frowned. "But last I heard, she was to marry
the lord of Norwood."

The old woman cackled. "My, you have been away
awhile. Lord Norwood up and disappeared about a
year ago. His cousin from up north inherited his castle, but Lady Elfrieda would not have a thing to do
with him. Now though, her father, Lord Ashford, has
died, and if she is to keep the castle and lands, she
must marry. So she has called a tournament and de-
clared she will marry the winner."

24

Gina smiled. "That does sound like it should bring quite a crowd."

Nodding, the woman went back to her work. "Aye, Gypsies, and merchants, and players, and who knows what-all from five shires around, more than like. I'll be taking baskets to sell myself. The tournament starts day after tomorrow."

"Thank you, old mother," Gina said with a curtsy. "May your baskets sell well."

Eagerly Gina began walking down the road, leaving Kevin standing at the crossroads. Then she turned, looked at him, and walked back.

"Kevin," she said hesitantly, "you would be better off staying with me at first. I know how it is to be suddenly dragged from your own world and dropped in another. And I am sorry. But not believing it will not make it any less real." She headed back up the road, and after a moment Kevin stumbled after her.

He felt more numb than anything else and scarcely noticed the ox carts, barefoot monks, or men on horseback that occasionally joined them on the dusty road. But the village itself was harder to ignore.

A higgledy-piggledy cluster of thatched buildings, one or two stories high, crowded together to form a maze of streets. Filthy streets, some dirt and some cobbled, all were now crowded with horses and wagons and people setting up booths. It looked to Kevin like a larger, messier, and much smellier version of the faire he'd been at a couple of hours earlier. Except, of course, that at one end of the main street was a stone church and at the other rose a very large, very real-looking stone castle.

Kevin closed his eyes, fighting down panic. After all, this should be very exciting. After years of studying the Middle Ages, Kevin was seeing the real thing. His mind shied away from tender questions like: How did this happen? How long will it last? Trying to feel interested and excited, he followed Gina through the streets.

The air was thick with the odor of horse droppings, sewage, sweat, garlic, and the sickly sweet smell coming from the fly-specked meat hanging in butchers' stalls. And through the cloud of odors, the air vibrated with noise. People talked and laughed, dogs barked, and merchants called their wares. A mule brayed raucously while two men yelled about how the beast was sitting down and blocking the road. There were no sweetly sung madrigals by ladies in filmy polyester dresses.

Kevin's calm began to crack. Finally he tapped Gina on the shoulder. "This is all very quaint and interesting, and it was kind of you to bring me along, but maybe I should be getting back. Could you please send me home now?"

"Send you? Squire Kevin, I have no more idea how I got back here than I do about how I was sent away. I made a place for myself in your world. You will just have to do the same in mine."

"But I don't—" A sudden thought hit him, and with a last grasp at suspicion he said, "Hey, how come I can understand everybody? In the Middle Ages they spoke English that was so funny, it might as well have been a foreign language."

Gina shrugged. "How would I know? When I landed in your world, there were some strange phrases used, but still I could understand most people. It must be part of the evil magic, so don't bother your mind with it."

Just then a tall, gangly man stepped from behind a large, brightly painted wagon. With a grin he hugged Gina.

"Ah, my little Gypsy princess. Where have you been? Our company has met your family three times this year, and they are always distraught and ask if we have seen you."

"Oh, Clarence!" Gina cried happily. "How good to see someone I know! Yes, it was dreadful. I got magicked to a truly frightful world and only now escaped—bringing this sorry fellow with me." She gestured to Kevin, then continued. "Is my family here?"

"Not yet, but they are bound to be soon. This is too big an event to miss. We have already put on two shows and almost filled a hat with coins."

Another member of the acting company climbed out of the wagon, wearing a tattered purple dress and struggling to tie on a yarn wig. As Gina was greeting him, there was a commotion up the street, and Kevin looked to see several mounted men forcing their way through the crowd. Two held lances from which hung red-and-black banners. Behind them rode several men in armor draped with red-and-black surcoats.

Gina, too, was staring at the riders. Pointing to the blond, mustached man in the middle, she whispered furiously, "That one, that snake! He's the villain who magicked me away when I stole his wretched jewels."

Kevin's mouth dropped open. He had seen that man once today already. It was the foppish blond lord whom Despard the Despicable had nearly hacked apart. The one who had lost the blue jewel.

4

Kevin the Demon

Clarence the actor pulled Gina back into the crowd, whispering, "If that man has a grievance against you, child, better stay out of sight. That's Sir Bertram, the new lord of Norwood, the one who wants to marry Lady Elfrieda except that she will not have him."

"Good for her!" Gina spat. "If only I could do something to make him as miserable as he has made me." An angry gleam flashed in her eyes. "In fact, I think I might try something right now." She left the players and at a cautious distance followed the mounted group down the road.

The tall actor laughed and slapped Kevin on the shoulder. "One thing Gypsies have a talent for is revenge. You now, lad, I can tell you are not one of her folk, but if she is a friend, I suggest that you follow to see that she does not get into any more trouble than she can wriggle out of."

Kevin hardly considered Gina a friend, but he had every intention of following. Not only had this Sir

Bertram of Norwood sent Gina into the future, he had been there himself today just before the two of them had slipped into the past. If there was any way for him to get home, Kevin figured, that blond knight might be the key.

Trotting down the rutted dusty street, Kevin dodged wagons, animals, and people that looked and smelled like dirtier versions of those at his own faire. A person could make a fortune around here, Kevin thought, selling deodorant or wash-and-wear fabric. Quickly he veered out of the way of a woman pouring a foul-smelling pot into the street. His foot landed in a heap of rotting garbage, stirring up a cloud of flies. Bug spray wouldn't hurt either, he thought, or perhaps a city street department. He wondered how many tourists those Renaissance faires would draw if they tried to be this realistic.

Crossing the lowered drawbridge, Kevin looked down, expecting to see a moat filled with deep, dark water. Instead the ditch was dry and littered with trash from the village, which for years, it seemed, had been growing around the castle walls. Animals that looked a lot like rats scurried among the broken pots and other trash. He guessed this wasn't a time when castles worried much about being attacked.

Once inside the walled courtyard, he looked around uneasily for Gina. With relief he saw her lounging in a shadowed corner, eyeing the group of men who had just ridden in. There were several such groups in the large courtyard, knights, squires, and men-at-arms. Kevin guessed that they must have come for the tournament. The place smelled of horse droppings and of the straw that had been strewn about in a weak attempt to keep the horses from churning the courtyard into a muddy mess.

Trying not to gape like a tourist, Kevin walked over to join Gina. She just nodded and kept listening to the men in red-and-black livery. With Sir Bertram having apparently gone inside, his men seemed to feel free to gossip about him.

"True," one said, "but I think Bertram hopes he can still persuade Lady Elfrieda to marry him. He is not a man to take no for an answer."

Another older man laughed. "Then he had better start learning how to. Elfrieda may have been set on marrying the lord of Norwood, but it was Sir Despard she had in mind, not his cousin, Bertram. They say that when Despard disappeared, so did the Norwood betrothal token, some old family medallion, and now the lovely lady of Ashford is using that as an excuse for not marrying Norwood's new lord."

"Care to speculate any more about what happened to the last lord?"

"No, I would not," the older man snapped, looking around uneasily. "And neither should you if you want to stay on at Norwood."

Just then an overworked-looking young groom hurried up to lead the horses to the stable, and the men headed inside. Excitedly Kevin turned to Gina.

"Did you hear that? Sir Despard. Do you think it's the same one?"

"As who?"

"As Despard the Despicable. That's not exactly a common name."

"Not in your world, maybe," Gina said, tossing her hair. Then she thought a moment. "But, yes, it could be the same. In your world, my 'Gypsies' were not always at the same faires as that particular jousting troupe. But when I first saw them, their 'black knight' was a new one, and rumor had it he was a little odd and hard to get along with."

"Didn't that basket lady say the old lord of Norwood disappeared about a year ago?"

Gina's dark eyes narrowed. "I'll bet that rat, Bertram, magicked him away the same as he did me."

"So that he could get his cousin's castle and girlfriend, too." Kevin shook his head. "Despard may be despicable, all right, but that sort of thing could put anyone in a foul mood."

After a moment's silence a cunning smile spread over Gina's dark face. "And here I was, planning just to cut Bertram's saddle girth or something. But I can come up with a lot better revenge than that. Come on, let's find this Lady Elfrieda."

"Let's?"

"Suit yourself. Stay out here and hire on as a real

squire—if you can. I am going to see if I can make life a little worse for the noble lord of Norwood.''

With a sinking feeling, Kevin looked around the courtyard. All he knew about being a squire came from books and the pretend stuff his parents' club did. But these squires had probably been in training since they could walk. He hated to admit it, but sometimes pretend worlds had it all over real ones. Sighing, he followed Gina.

She led them through a dark doorway into some sort of storeroom. ''Do you know where you're going?'' Kevin whispered.

''I have never been in this castle, if that is what you mean. But the ladies' quarters will probably be in the newer part—that would be those towers on the right with the pointy windows. All we need to do is find some stairs and go up.''

''Without getting caught.''

''Of course.''

Kevin stumbled after Gina across the dim, object-filled room to a door on the far side. From there they peered into a large, high-ceilinged hall furnished with benches and several long tables. It was empty except at the far end, where people who looked like servants were carrying trays and baskets.

''Let's be servants,'' Gina whispered.

After poking around the shadowy storeroom and disturbing a couple of squeaking rats, she handed Kevin a basket of what appeared to be squash seeds and picked up a wooden box of thick yellowish candles for herself. "Come on and act like you are supposed to be here."

Gina stepped out, and, meekly lowering her head, she walked purposefully across the high open space toward an arched doorway. Ducking his head, Kevin tried to copy her every movement. The stone floor was strewn with rushes that crackled underfoot and smelled a little like the herb shelf at home—and a little more like the garbage pail. Kevin expected to hear someone cry out for them to stop at any instant. No one did.

They passed under the arch. Without a word, Gina hurried to the base of a stone stairway and started up.

The wedge-shaped stairs spiraled upward and were so narrow at the inside that Kevin's feet could scarcely fit. He kept close to the rough stone wall of the stairwell, hating to think what would happen if they met someone coming down.

Then they did hear voices coming from above, but before they bumped into the speakers, they saw an opening onto the first-floor landing. Gina and Kevin scurried into a corridor just in time to miss two soldiers who, arguing amicably about the coming tournament, passed the landing and continued down.

As Kevin started tiptoeing back to the stairs, Gina grabbed his arm and pointed out of an arched window. There was no glass, but the wooden shutters were partially open, and through the sunlit arch they could see where a wall of the castle turned outward and ended in a round tower.

"I would guess that Elfrieda's rooms are there. See, the building is in the latest fashion, and it overlooks the herb garden and the river. If I were a lady and had to stay cooped up in one spot, that is where I would choose."

Kevin had to admit, the view was nice. If he pretended, it could almost be Indiana. Almost, but not quite. He smiled grudgingly. Things could be worse. He could have ended up on one of those medieval battlefields where guys hack off each other's arms and legs—for real.

Together they wound their way through a maze of corridors and up more spiral stairs. Whenever they met someone else, they either ducked around corners or walked by as if someone had sent out an urgent order for squash seeds and candles.

Finally they heard two women's voices from a room up ahead. Gina gestured for them to hide behind the half-open door, and they crouched, listening, in its shadow.

"The train of your green gown needs mending, my lady. Would you not rather wear the blue?"

"No, I would rather you mended the green and not argue." Then came a bitter-sounding laugh. "Actually I would as soon wear black to this tournament, for all that I am likely to enjoy the outcome. There is not one knight in the running who I would rather see win over another.''

"Oh, come, my lady, some would make quite fine husbands. Really, you cannot mourn Sir Despard forever.''

"I can and I will. Every time his sniveling cousin comes to ask for my hand, it reminds me how much Sir Bertram of Norwood is *not* Sir Despard of Norwood. Thank the good Lord he does not have the family medallion or, to keep my word, I would have to marry the beast.''

"Be that as it may,'' the older voice continued, ''a black gown will simply not do for a tournament. So if my lady will excuse me, I will go fetch some more green thread.''

"Yes, and do take your time, Matilda. I would as soon be alone awhile.''

The wooden door suddenly opened further, pressing the two eavesdroppers back against the wall. Footsteps and the swishing of skirts faded away. Boldly Gina stepped from their hiding place and walked into the room. Kevin did not want to follow but knew he'd feel even sillier if he stayed in the hall, cowering.

Lady Elfrieda, wearing a pale gray gown, was sitting in front of an open window. The view through the double arches showed green meadows and a winding, tree-lined river. Afternoon sun glowed in her coppery hair and on the woven figures that were worked into the tapestry hanging on the wall. Startled, the young woman looked up from her embroidery and stared at the children.

"Did I send for you?"

"Not in so many words, my lady," Gina said in a low, mysterious voice. "But your heart has called out for the words that we bring."

"Oh," Elfrieda said in an annoyed tone, "Gypsies. Well, I really don't need my fortune told today, thank you."

"Ah, but you do, or at least you need your fortune mended. For I know what has become of Sir Despard, your beloved."

"You do?" The lady stood up, embroidery falling unheeded to the floor. "Where is he?"

"Even now," Gina intoned, "he dwells in a land of demons and strange devices."

"How? How is this possible?"

"Sorcery, my lady, evil sorcery. And it is his own black-hearted cousin, Sir Bertram, who magicked him there."

Elfrieda stifled a squeal behind raised hands. Then she paced across the room, turning suddenly back to face them. "I would not put such a thing past that snake. But why should I believe *you*? How could two mere children know of such things?"

"Ah, my lady," Gina said, dramatically stepping forward and clutching the woman's pale hands. "We know because we ourselves have just this day escaped from that same demon world. I was sent there a year ago when I chanced to anger Sir Bertram, but Kevin here is a reformed demon, a native of that world. He wanted so much to live in a world like ours that he finally fled here.''

Kevin flushed. Oh, great, he thought. Now he was Kevin the Demon instead of Kevin the Squire. And he hadn't even read any books about that trade.

5

Damsel in Distress

Lady Elfrieda's blue eyes widened, and her pale complexion grew even paler. "A demon?" she whispered. Then her face seemed to harden into resolution, and she took a step forward. "Then, young sir, if you have indeed given that over, I welcome you. But tell me of this world of yours. Is it unbearably dreadful? Has my poor Despard come to harm there?"

"Well, it's not really all *that* dreadful. But I suppose that Despard the—that Sir Despard was pretty shaken up when he first got there. It is awfully different. Still, he did find a way to make a living, though wanting to get back here all the time must have made him pretty foul-tempered."

"Oh, my poor little darling," Elfrieda moaned. Kevin wondered how anyone could think of huge, surly Despard the Despicable as a "little darling."

Clasping and unclasping her hands, the lady paced in front of the window. "But I should not be surprised that Bertram should do such a thing. Not after what must have happened to old Cuthbert.''

Kevin and Gina looked at each other and sat on a cushioned bench. ''What happened to old Cuthbert?'' they asked together.

''Cuthbert was a friend of my father's. They fought together in the Crusades. When they returned from the Holy Land, Cuthbert came to live with us. He fancied himself something of an alchemist, and he had a little tower room, where he did some rather odd things.

''Oh, he was harmless enough, though he would go away for days at a time and return suddenly with no one seeing his coming or going. And he brought back some very strange things indeed. Father Clovis thought that these were surely devices of the devil, but I cannot really think so. Cuthbert was a good-hearted old man, for all that he was a little crotchety.''

''Yeah, but what does this have to do with that Bertram guy?'' Kevin asked.

Elfrieda sat down again in her chair by the window. ''Well, you see, about two years ago Bertram came down from his estate in the north to visit his cousin Despard and us as well. His father had also been with mine in the Crusades. That was when the swine first asked me to marry him. I told him it was impossible since I had already given my love, and Despard had pledged me the family betrothal medallion.

"But while he was here, Bertram took an interest in old Cuthbert and the mysterious doings in his tower. I think the old fellow was flattered, and they spent a lot of time together. Then one day Cuthbert disappeared and never returned. That was about the time I noticed that Bertram was wearing the jeweled belt Cuthbert had always worn—the one he had brought back from the Holy Land—the one he claimed was magic."

"That belt!" Gina interrupted. "That is what I slipped off Bertram before he chased me down for it and magicked me off to that awful world of Kevin's."

Kevin said nothing. His mind was jostling bits and pieces together. That jeweled belt had lost a link when the two men fought by the jousting lists. He had picked it up, slipped it into his pouch, and then had it with him when he and Gina had somehow been sent back here.

Fumbling with the pouch strings, he reached past the video game and a handful of coins until his fingers touched the gold-set jewel. He pulled it out.

"Did the jewels in the belt look like this?"

Gina gasped. "They did! That is part of the same belt."

Elfrieda reached for it and held it up against the blazing sunset. The jewel glowed like a drop of deep blue ocean, and the entwining gold leaves seemed to run with fire. "It is a link from Cuthbert's belt. Perhaps, if it was magic, as he claimed, then those times

41

when he disappeared, he could have been using that belt to visit worlds like Demon Kevin's."

"And," Gina added, "Bertram could have tricked Cuthbert into showing him how to use the jewels and then sent Cuthbert away, like he did to me and Despard."

Kevin smiled broadly, taking back the jewel. "And maybe they don't all have to be linked together to work. If a single jewel sent us here, maybe I can use this one to get back home, if I knew how the magic worked."

"I thought you wanted to come here," Elfrieda said.

Kevin cleared his throat, thinking he had better keep his stories straight. "Oh, sure, of course, for a visit. But I really would like to get home now."

"I suspect that if we looked through that old tower of Cuthbert's," Gina said, "we could find something that would tell us how to use the jewels."

"Perhaps," Elfrieda said thoughtfully. Then she picked up her embroidery and began plucking at it nervously before saying, "All right, I will let you both into Cuthbert's tower so you can sort through his secrets. But there is something I would like you to do for me first."

Kevin didn't like the sound of this.

"What is your bargain, my lady?" Gina asked evenly.

Elfrieda blushed. "Please do not think ill of me to bargain like a merchant. But I am desperately afraid.

Foolishly I told Bertram that I would only marry a lord of Norwood who presented me with the family medallion. I felt sure it was safe from him. But one of my maids learned from a Norwood guard that Bertram has been practically tearing the place apart looking for something. I know where Despard must have hidden it, and if Bertram is being that thorough, he may find it. Then I would be duty-bound to marry him no matter who wins the tournament."

"So," Gina said, "you want us to go to Norwood, find the medallion, and bring it back to you."

"Yes, I do."

"Swell, but I really want to go home now," Kevin put in.

Gina glared at him. "And I really want my revenge on Sir Bertram. Of course, you can always try using the jewel yourself and see if it sends you home."

"Right. And it might also send me back to a swamp full of dinosaurs or something. I'd rather find an instruction book first, thank you."

"Then you will just have to find Lady Elfrieda's medallion before that."

Kevin sighed. Well, he might as well play chivalrous as if this medieval stuff was real—because it was. And it was likely to stay that way for him unless he went through with this bargain.

"Sure, count me in, I guess. So, where do you think this medallion is hidden, Miss . . . Lady Elfrieda?"

"First you—"

"My lady!" the maid said from the doorway. "Who are these children?"

"Oh, Matilda, you startled me. These are . . . these are Gypsies I had bring some ingredients I need for a love potion. If I am to have a husband, day after tomorrow, I might as well start out right."

The maid eyed the things Kevin and Gina had laid on a table. "Candles and squash seeds in a love potion?"

"Oh yes, mistress," Gina said with a curtsy. "An old Romany love potion. Very powerful."

"Humph. Well, it had better be, and you may want to take it yourself, my lady. I hear that Sir Bertram has just ridden back to his castle. Rumor has it that he has come up with a new idea of where to look for that medallion."

"Oh no!" Elfrieda wailed. "We may be too late. Hurry, Matilda, go bid John the stable boy to saddle up Windy and Trouble. I must send these two youngsters off right away."

"But—"

"Go, do it!"

The maid curtsied and left. Looking around the room as if the walls might be listening, Elfrieda sat down beside the children on the bench.

"At Norwood Castle, there is an old part built even before the time of William the Conqueror. A square tower, one room above the other with a parapet on top. That was where Despard and I used to play as children. The bottom room was our dungeon, the second room our Great Hall, and the top the battlements where we held off enemies. There are four carvings around the base of the parapet wall: a boar, an eagle, a lion, and a swan. The boar's stone is loose, and we used to hide special treasures behind it. I am sure that is where Despard would have kept the medallion. Go bring it to me, and I will help you with Cuthbert's things or in any other way I can."

Gina stood up. "It is a bargain, my lady, and as good as done."

Kevin looked a little doubtful. Gina scowled at him. "Come now, Kevin the Demon Squire. Your people spend their time dreaming of medieval adventure. Would you pass up a chance to go on a real quest when it is offered you?"

Kevin fought back a grin for a moment, then quit trying. "Put that way, how can I refuse?"

6

Castle Norwood

Night had fallen by the time they rode out of the stable. Kevin had deliberately not taken the horse named Trouble. He wasn't *that* good a rider.

Now, as they pounded over the dark, uneven roads, Kevin found his excitement over this quest quickly fading. The air felt damp and heavy as if it were deciding whether or not to rain. Although Lady Elfrieda had said Norwood was only a few hours away, it had already been an exhausting day—in both centuries. And now, with every jolting second, Kevin wanted more and more just to be in bed—his bed. He didn't even want to be dreaming this.

He was practically asleep in the saddle when Gina, who had been riding ahead, pulled up and waved him to a halt. "There are people camped beside the road ahead. If they are outlaws, that could be trouble, because with these horses we now have something worth stealing. Do you have any weapons with you?"

"No," Kevin said, disgusted. He hadn't even worn

a plastic dagger with his costume. All he had was a video game and a dead digital watch.

"Well," she said with a toss of her dark hair, "we will just have to put a bold face on it. Besides, they are probably not robbers but only travelers on their way to the tournament."

Cautiously they rode past, eyes straining through the dark trees to see the firelit people, wagons, and horses that were camped beyond. Suddenly Gina squealed. She swerved her horse off the road and headed right into their camp.

"Mother! Father! It's me, Gina! I'm home!"

Gypsies, not outlaws, Kevin realized with relief. He tugged Windy to a halt. Well, at least one of them was home.

But soon he, too, was swept up in the homecoming. Everybody was talking, laughing, and crying at once. And there were a lot of everybodies. Kevin finally counted a mother, a mustached father, a grandmother, a large uncle, two, possibly three aunts, and a shifting number of young people who were either sisters, brothers, or cousins. There were also cats and dogs and a pet owl who sat on Gina's shoulders, rubbing its fluffy white head against her cheek.

Gina told her story with many dramatic additions. The others were so impressed about Kevin being a runaway demon that he almost wished he were. On inspiration, he brought out his pocket video game and astounded everyone with the flashings and beepings of this authentic "demon box." He was a little puzzled that it should work while his watch didn't, but he finally decided that it might be because it was time that had changed and not the principles of electricity.

Despite being the center of attention, he was not sorry when Gina said there wasn't time to make merry all night. Over a big meal she explained about the quest that Lady Elfrieda had sent them on. With much solemn oath taking, the others agreed that it was now their family duty to seek revenge as well. While Kevin and Gina were given places to sleep in one of the wagons, the whole gathering packed up and set off, not for Ashford but for Norwood.

Kevin figured that, tired though he was, he could never get to sleep wrapped in a smelly, flea-infested blanket in the back of a jolting wagon—especially with Hearn, Gina's round-eyed pet owl, watching them from its swaying perch. It was well after dawn, however, when he woke to find them camped in a meadow outside a large, brooding castle.

While breakfasting on bread, berries, and cold chicken, they watched the castle drawbridge being lowered for the day. It wasn't long before several guards in red and black strolled out and asked their business.

Gina's father explained that they had just camped there for the night on their way to Ashford but they would be happy to pay for their stay by telling fortunes, or mending pots and pans, or perhaps Gina's mother, sister, and a girl cousin or two could dance. By now the crowd of guards was growing, and this last suggestion raised boisterous approval. Gina's father and uncle brought out flute and drum, and the diversion began.

Kevin wanted to see how the real thing compared to the jingly belly dancing of his time, but according to plan he and Gina sauntered away from the crowd and then slipped through the now unguarded gate into the castle grounds.

He looked around, impressed. His second real medieval castle in as many days. But this one, with no village around it, seemed even darker and gloomier. At least they didn't have to go sneaking around inside. Their goal was obvious. In a far, neglected-looking part of the large walled-in grounds rose a squat tower, part of an older building, most of which was now gone. The safest way to reach it looked to be by creeping along the base of the newer buildings' walls, where no one ought to be able to glance out and see them.

As they finally drew nearer to the old tower, they heard voices and an occasional thumping crash.

"Sounds like Elfrieda was right," Gina whispered. "Bertram must have guessed that Despard hid the medallion in his old play tower. I pray we are not too late."

"Well, from all that racket, it sounds like they're still looking and are still on one of the lower floors.

But how are we going to get them out so we can sneak up to the top?''

"I suppose I could start dancing," Gina said doubtfully.

"Hmm, maybe . . . Wait, I know. The demon box!"

Kevin pulled the video game from the pouch at his belt. Flipping open the back, he unhooked the batteries, then jammed several of the keys in the down position by wedging in bits of straw he'd picked up from the ground. Feeling like a movie commando, he gestured for Gina to follow as he dashed toward the little tower.

Placing the game on a fallen rock at the tower's base, Kevin snapped the batteries back in. With Gina at his heels, he pelted around to the castle's far side as a loud and totally out-of-place beeping rose behind them. Soon, too, they heard voices from inside.

"What is that unearthly row?"

"I know not, my lord."

"Well, go see."

Stomping footsteps were followed by, "Most strange, my lord. Some work of the devil. Come see for yourself. I dare not touch it."

There was cursing; then there were two more sets of footsteps.

When the tower seemed empty, Kevin and Gina slipped inside and up the ladder to the second floor. They looked around, then saw an unlocked wooden door and dashed through it and up the steep stone steps to the tower's top. For a moment they dropped to the paving stones, panting and giggling. Then they set about looking for the stone boar. Soon they had found all four carvings, but though they could easily pick out the eagle and swan, the stone was too worn to easily tell boar from lion. Finally they chose the one with the shortest tail and began prying at it.

At first nothing moved; then slowly the stone began to wiggle like a loose tooth. It popped out so suddenly, they were sent rolling onto their backs. Eagerly Gina scrambled back and reached inside. In moments a golden chain was dangling from her fingers, gleaming in the morning sun. At its end swung a flat gold disk with somebody's head stamped on it. Kevin thought it looked really old—older than medieval, anyway, so that meant *old*.

He was just leaning forward for a better look when a gloved hand reached from behind him and snatched the medallion away.

Both children spun around. Sir Bertram of Norwood stood above them. A breeze fluttered the blond hair about his shoulders, and the familiar jeweled belt glinted at his waist. Beneath his mustache his mouth curved into a sneer.

"Thank you both for saving me the trouble of demolishing the entire tower for this. Don't I know you?" He squinted down at Gina. "Ah yes, the little Gypsy thief I sent off to Despard's place. When I saw the nature of that beeping thing outside, I suspected someone had slipped back from there. How did you manage it?"

Kevin tried to look as blank as the stones around him.

Bertram studied the two of them. "You found the belt link I lost, didn't you?"

Silence.

"Give it back, now!"

More silence.

Like a hawk, the man swooped down. Grabbing Gina's wrist, he swung her up and over the edge of the parapet. Shrieking, she dangled from his grasp like a helpless kitten.

"Give me that jewel, wench, or I will drop you down to feed the crows."

For a second Kevin hesitated; then he pulled the single jewel from his pouch. "Here. Put her down safely, and you can have it."

Surprised, Bertram turned back to look at him. Then, with a harsh laugh, he swung the girl back inside the parapet and dumped her in a heap on the stones. With a mock bow, he took the offered jewel; then, plucking several loose, heavy threads from his tunic, he tied the link securely to the dangling end of his belt.

"That will do until I can visit a goldsmith. But just now, thanks to your timely assistance, I must be off to claim my bride."

The confident sneer returned to his face as he looked Kevin over. "Were you worth the bother, I would wonder how you fit into this, boy. But you will not be around long enough to matter. I could send you two off in time again, except that there you would have a much better life than you deserve. So I think I will lock you up here. I would hate to cheat the carrion crows completely."

With that, he hung the medallion's gold chain around his own neck and tromped down the stairs, closing and locking the thick oak door at the bottom.

Like an omen, a large black crow cawed from the sky overhead.

7

Durance Vile

Through clenched teeth, Gina said, "I will not give that donkey's turd the satisfaction of hearing me yell and bang on the door."

Kevin couldn't agree more, but as soon as they heard Bertram and his men leave the tower, he and Gina hurried to the bottom of the steps and tried pushing, prying, and pulling at the door. Nothing budged. And the stones around the door proved just as solid.

Once back on top, they peered over the parapet, studying the walls on all sides. "Only a lizard could climb down that way," Gina muttered.

"Do we have enough stuff to tie together so we can lower ourselves down?" Kevin asked. But when the answer proved to be two belts, a shawl, and a hair ribbon, they abandoned that idea.

"Not much point, I suppose, in yelling and waving to get someone's attention," Kevin said.

Gina shook her head. "Whether they like him or

not, everyone here is bound to their lord, and if Sir Bertram wants to leave two children to starve to death on a tower, they will look the other way and let him do it.''

Discouraged, the two slumped down against the shadowed part of the wall and sank into thought. Kevin's mind filled with the picture of crows perching on a couple of sun-bleached skeletons. At times he had given thought to how he might die someday, but it usually involved something heroic or dramatic at least. Starving to death and being eaten by birds centuries before he was born had never come into the picture.

Around midday they heard a commotion. Peering over the parapet, they saw Sir Bertram and a party of men-at-arms preparing to ride from the castle. If Kevin's mouth hadn't been so dry, he would have spit on them. ''There goes the top slime ball of the Middle Ages off to claim his stolen bride,'' he growled.

Gina snorted, then after a minute said, ''Maybe with all of them gone, it will be easier to catch someone's attention.''

''I thought you said there wasn't any point in that.''

''Not the castle folk, I mean my people. They must know something is wrong, or we would be back by now. If we can let them know where we are, maybe they can help.''

''How? I mean, sure, there are a lot of them, but hardly enough to storm a castle, even if most of the guards are at a neighbor's tournament.''

"As they say where you come from, 'Give me a break, will you?' My people are Romany. They will come up with something smarter than that."

"What?"

"I don't know," she answered in a wavering voice.

Still, after the last of Bertram's troops had ridden out, Gina stood up, leaned against the parapet, and began to sing. Other than its being a very odd thing to do at the time, Kevin didn't mind. Gina's voice was as clear as the hand bells at church, and the tune was simple and catchy. Even the words seemed right: about a caged bird that yearned to be free. After a time sitting with his legs in the sun and his back in shadow, he began to drift asleep. Fitfully he'd wake at the sound of a crow cawing and then lapse into wondering if they would die of thirst or starvation first. He'd read that thirst was the worst. From the cottony way his mouth felt, he could believe it.

For a while he must have fallen into deeper sleep, because when Kevin woke next, the sun had moved well to the west, and he was all in shadow. Gina's song was being echoed from far out in the woods. A bird? He stood up and leaned against the wall beside her.

Beyond the outer castle wall, where meadow met woods, they could see a figure waving a bright cloth.

"They know where we are now," Gina rasped. "Good thing, because I have just about used up my voice."

"Well done," Kevin said, feeling a little guilty at having slept through it all. "But what good's that likely to do us?"

Wearily Gina sat down in the lengthening shadow of the western wall. "I don't know. The rest is up to them." She shot him a weakly defiant glare. "They *are* Romany. They will come up with something."

Soon she had slipped off to sleep, but Kevin knew he'd had all the sleep he could squeeze out. Time crawled. He didn't even have his video game. Nothing to do but think. But his thoughts kept circling back to his home. Even his parents' endless pretending didn't seem so bad now. It was part of what made his world real, after all, and was as real as any of the rest of it. Suddenly his throat got so thick, he thought he'd choke. He made himself lean back and figure out what shape the clouds looked like.

He watched and imagined until the clouds started turning orange and pink with sunset. Then stiffly he stood up and watched the sun drop behind the dark, wooded hills. Lovely, but he could scarcely enjoy the view. There was no way he wanted to spend the night locked in a ruined medieval tower—let alone what might be the rest of a very short life.

He almost screamed as something swooped down at him from the darkening sky. "Not ready for you yet, crow!" he yelled at the thing circling the tower. But it wasn't black. It was white.

Sleepily Gina stood up beside him. Then she

squealed and stretched an arm into the air. "Hearn! Hearn, come down. Come!"

Kevin watched as the great white owl circled once more. Wrapping an arm in her shawl, Gina stretched it out again. The bird glided down, then abruptly shot out its legs and landed on its mistress's arm.

"Oh, good old bird," Gina said, nuzzling its feathers. "So you have come to save us, have you?"

"I hate to dampen this happy reunion," Kevin said, "but I don't think that bird can carry us down."

"Of course not, lackwit, but he can carry this." Swiftly Gina unbound the red ribbon from her hair and tied it to one of the owl's scaly legs. Then she flung her arm upward. The owl took off, circled once, and glided off toward the dark, ragged line of trees.

Kevin let his questions go unasked. Shrugging, he sat down in the growing cold and watched the stars coming out one by one in the evening sky. They looked like the ones he'd always watched from home. A few centuries didn't make much difference to stars, he figured.

The sky was aglitter with stars when Kevin saw a dark shape sweep across them. Beside him, Gina jumped up and gave a liquid hooting call. It was answered from above. Then, with a flutter of white wings, the owl was on her arm again.

It looked as if the bird had grown an extremely long tail. Something snaky was trailing down from him, across the floor of the tower, and over the wall.

Kevin peered closer and realized that several bright hair ribbons now adorned the owl's leg, and they were all tied to the end of a rope.

Gina laughed and stroked the bird's downy breast. "What a wily old fellow you are, and strong, too. All that rope must weigh a lot."

They soon had the rope untied and their end looped around one of the raised stones in the wall's crenulations. At last his stint in Boy Scouting was coming in handy, Kevin thought as he tied a double half-hitch knot. He looked over the edge, but by starlight it was hard to tell how far down the rope dangled. Still, it had to get a lot nearer the ground than they were now.

"Want to be first?" Kevin asked, uncertain what was proper in this case and equally uncertain if he cared.

"Yes, thank you," Gina said, giving her arm a decisive shake. The owl jumped onto the parapet and sat watching them like a white gargoyle. Nimbly Gina climbed up, grasped the rope, and lowered herself over like someone used to scaling walls by rope.

Kevin was feeling suddenly unwell. This had been the part of Boy Scouting he had liked least, the rock-climbing badge. But now his end of the rope was jerking, showing Gina was down, and before he could think any more about it, he made himself climb up and over the edge. His mind was then so filled with the mechanics of moving hands and feet that there was little room for feeling the yawning, fearful emptiness stretching behind him. Not, at least, until he was on the ground, and his legs suddenly felt like overcooked noodles.

Gina allowed him little rest. Flapping silently above them, the owl launched itself into the night, and she began following its route as it soared above the abandoned stretch of castle grounds and disappeared over the outer wall. Kevin didn't think much of an owl as a guide, but he hadn't any better route to suggest, so he followed, trying to be as silent and shadowlike as he could.

As they neared the outer wall, he strained his eyes in the starlit darkness. He could just make out a wooden ladder leading up to the wall's parapet. Gina had reached the base when a voice froze them like statues. "Ho, who is moving down there?"

Kevin looked up along the wall. Faint movement, starlight glinting off armor. A guard. Why, Kevin chided himself, had they acted as if the general defenses were abandoned in this old part of the castle? Both children pressed themselves flat against the wall as the voice called again.

"Come, I saw you. Who is it? Speak or I will call other guards."

Kevin felt sick with fear. Maybe he should meow like a cat. It was an overused trick, but at least this guard wouldn't have seen it in all the movies. As he opened his mouth, Gina suddenly flung her arms around him.

"Oh, please," she cried, "don't call the others. My boyfriend and I were just trying to find someplace private."

"Ha, I should have guessed," came the gruff reply. "The others get the tournament, and I get scullery maids and stable boys."

"Oh, you will not tell, will you?"

"Not if you choose someone else's watch next time. Need I say 'good night' to you, or can you manage to have one on your own?" The coarse laugh gradually faded as the guard marched back along the wall.

Kevin was glad the darkness hid his fiery blush. Disentangling himself from Gina's arms and ignoring her smug giggles, he looked up to the wall. The shadowy guard, still moving away, reached, then passed, a small square tower.

"The guard's out of sight now," he whispered. "Should we climb up?"

"No. This is where Hearn flew over, but we had better stay back against the wall and wait."

"Wait for what?"

The answer came in a faint swish through the air and a clatter on the stony ground. Gina dashed toward the spot. In the pale starlight, Kevin thought he saw something stretching like a cobweb back up and over the wall. A rope! In seconds Gina was back, holding the arrow to which it was tied.

Kevin whistled softly. "Better than Robin Hood."

Gina sniffed and started to reply, but Kevin quickly

added, "I know, I know. That Robin Hood guy's just some upstart from Nottinghamshire. But he *does* have the best publicity agent. Now, do we go up the ladder?"

Gina led the way, and soon they had repeated the rope-climbing scene and were standing outside the castle walls. An owl hooted from woods nearby, and, like two hunted deer, they ran toward the spot.

Kevin almost screamed when a huge man stepped out of the trees and hugged them both like a hungry bear. But soon Gina's uncle was leading them to where the Gypsies and their wagons waited in the woods. Within a few minutes their tale of failed vengeance had been told, and everyone agreed that to redeem their Romany honor, some new attempt must be made to trouble Sir Bertram of Norwood.

As Kevin spent his second night in a swaying, flea-infested, and very crowded wagon, it was not honor he was concerned about. Nor, he had to admit, was he fretting over the lovely young Lady Elfrieda's having to marry the villainous Sir Bertram.

It was Bertram's belt he was thinking about. Because if he couldn't get ahold of it and figure out how to use it, he might be spending a good many more nights in a medieval Gypsy wagon.

8

On the Fields of Combat

Unable to sleep in more than snatches, Kevin finally joined Gina's quiet, mustached father on the wagon box. Huddled under a blanket against the cold, they watched a graying dawn spread over the fields and woods of old England. Only now it wasn't *old* England. In fact, Kevin realized, "now" was always "now" no matter when it was. And this was now's England. Still, this was not where or when he belonged.

They arrived in time to see the rising sun light the steeple of Ashford's church and turn the white banners above the castle to gold. Already a crowd on foot, wagon, and horseback was trickling into the village to take part in the day's faire and tournament. Gina's father led the wagons to a spot near the riverside meadow.

A large area had been roped off for the tournament, and spectators were already staking out their places. At one side of the lists, a raised wooden platform had been set up and covered with a white-and-gold canopy. Except for a few servants arranging chairs, it was still empty.

"So now what?" Kevin asked Gina as she joined him on the wagon seat while her father swung down to unharness the horses. The others were sleepily climbing out of their wagons to tend to the animals, make camp, and set up the booth where they would sell ribbons, bangles, and charms.

"Let's return Windy and Trouble to the castle stables. That will give us an excuse to get inside so we can find Elfrieda and tell her what happened."

"Yeah, and if the law worked properly around here," Kevin grumbled, "Bertram would be locked up for child abuse or attempted murder or something." Before Gina could snap out her reply, he added, "I know, I know. Things don't work that way these days. Nobles have all the rights, and kids haven't any. Let's get the horses."

The two Ashford horses had been tied behind one of the wagons and were now enjoying mouthfuls of dewy grass. Still they willingly followed the children and picked up speed as they neared their castle, stables, and morning oats.

The castle yard was bustling with activity, and the two young people were scarcely spared a glance. But once they delivered their horses, they were told that Lady Elfrieda was busy preparing for the tournament and couldn't possibly see them now. Twice they tried sneaking into the castle, and twice they were thrown out. Finally they made it as far as the corridor leading to the ladies' chambers, but glancing out the window, they saw Lady Elfrieda, her auburn hair set off by her green gown, as she, her ladies, and several other nobles walked across the meadow to the pavilion.

Hurriedly they retraced their steps. "So what's plan B?" Kevin asked as they pushed their way through the noisy, smelly, jostling crowd that surrounded the lists.

Gina frowned. "I would have said it was to get close enough to Elfrieda to tell her about the medallion, but doesn't that look like Sir Bertram sitting beside her now?"

"Yeah, which means she probably already knows about the medallion. But still, if we're going to have any kind of crack at that tower of old Cuthbert's, we'd better let her know that we tried, at least. Come on, if we can manage to sneak in and out of an enemy castle, surely we can get closer to an open pavilion."

They sidled as close as they could until guards in white-and-gold surcoats turned them back. For long minutes they hung around, looking for a chance to slip past. Suddenly a fistfight among several onlookers caught the closest guard's attention, and in moments Gina and Kevin were at the back of the platform, trying to look like meek and purposeful servants.

When the real servants craned to watch a new pair of knights passing toward the far end of the field, the two crouched down and ducked beneath the wooden platform. Bending low, they crept through the half dark until they were right below where Lady Elfrieda sat. Seated beside her, Sir Bertram seemed to be struggling to make conversation.

"It was good of you, my lady, to agree to go on with the tournament even though the question of your marriage is now already settled."

Silence.

"It would have disappointed the people if this show had been called off—to say nothing of the tournament contestants."

More silence.

Kevin squinted up between the floor planks and saw the blond knight tugging nervously at his mustache. Gruffly he cleared his throat.

"Well, I suppose I will have to offer today's victor a gold cup or something, since the chief prize, my lady's hand in marriage, has already been awarded."

The silence broke. "Sir Bertram. By some means or other, you obtained the medallion, and I did give my word of honor to marry he who bore that token. But, in good faith, I also gave my word to marry the winner of this contest. Therefore, it seems that the only honorable thing is to let the bearer of the medallion contend with the winner of the tournament for the 'prize,' as you call it."

The other laughed. "And perhaps you are now expecting me to reject that offer and forfeit the prize? Hardly likely, my lady. I am well versed in the arts of combat, some say the equal of my late lamented cousin. But even were that not so, I would have little fear of your terms. For you see, Norwood has entered a champion in this tournament, one of my retainers whose prowess is so monumental that I have every confidence in his winning. And were he to do so, he would, of course, yield his victor's claim to me as his liege lord. There, you can see him now—the large knight in green and brown. His name is Sir Brian of Beasley."

From where they crouched, Kevin and Gina peered around the rough posts holding the platform. The mounted contestants were gathering around the far end of the lists. There was a knight in brown and blue, one in red and white, and another all in yellow with several more milling around behind those. Their large, burly horses wore armor and trappings that matched in color those of their knights. Despite himself, Kevin was thrilled. This was the real thing.

Then he saw the knight in green and brown, and his excitement shriveled. The fellow was not just large, he was huge. His brown horse looked like a four-legged tank, and the rider, even without his armor, must have weighed at least three hundred pounds.

"Whew," Kevin whispered. "This Brian the

Beastly makes Despard the Despicable look like a minor wimp.''

"Size isn't everything," Gina said firmly. "Despard is big enough, but besides that, he knows what to do and when."

"Yeah, but he's also several hundred years and several thousand miles away."

Gina turned to him, determination building around her like a storm. "Then we must bring him here. If we can get hold of Bertram's jewels long enough to learn how to use them, we can go fetch Despard."

"Right!" Kevin said, grimly peering up through the cracks to where Sir Bertram was sitting. Maybe he could slip something up, hook it around the belt's dangling link, and yank the whole thing down here. Searching around beneath the platform, he found nothing but a few spindly twigs. What he needed was a good wire coat hanger, but they hadn't been invented yet. Then he got another idea and whispered it to Gina.

Soon they were out from beneath the platform and lounging around near some of the castle servants. Kevin spied one page about his size and strolled over to him.

"Why are you hanging around here?" he asked the boy innocently. "Don't you want to stand over by the side there and get a better look?"

"Of course I do, but my job is to bring out a tray

of wine whenever the noble folk in the pavilion get thirsty."

"Well, I tell you," Kevin said confidentially, "I am a squire. Sir David of Indiana is my knight, though he is not here yet. I've seen a lot of these tournaments—they're nothing to me. But I've never had a chance to take a close look at Lady Elfrieda. They say she is the most gorgeous thing in three shires. Suppose you let me wear your tabard for a bit and do your job while you slip forward for a better look at the contest?"

"Well, I don't know . . ."

"Look, I'll even give you some money. It's rare coinage from a distant land. My master brought it back from the Crusades. Sure to be worth quite a lot."

"Well . . ."

Kevin fumbled in his pouch and pulled out some coins he'd been planning to spend on snacks at the faire. Three quarters, a dime, two pennies, and a nickel. He hoped that the books were right about most kids in this time not being able to read. "United States of America" and the dates would take a lot of explanation. "Here, quite a fortune for you."

The boy hesitated; then, closing his fist over the coins, he slipped out of the white-and-gold tabard. Kevin pulled it over his own head and in moments was standing on the platform, tray of wine cups in hand. The tournament contestants were beginning their ceremonial ride past the pavilion.

"Wine, my lady?"

"Now?" Elfrieda said, looking up. She caught her breath as she recognized Kevin, the reformed young demon, but at his warning look she said nothing and took the cup. Then Kevin moved beside Sir Bertram.

As the man reached absently for his cup, Kevin grasped the last link in Bertram's jeweled belt and tugged.

The wine went flying, the knight was nearly jerked off his seat, but the lowest jeweled link came free. In seconds Kevin had jumped off the platform, and he and Gina were running along the edge of the crowd. Behind them, Bertram bellowed for guards to stop them.

Weaving and dodging like rabbits, they charged through a final wall of people, then pelted toward the village. Guards, swords drawn, were not far behind.

With the tournament beginning, the village was largely deserted, and the two children raced down one street after another, looking for somewhere to hide. Then they saw the players' wagon, with tall Clarence the actor sitting in front, repairing a costume.

"Clarence!" Gina gasped. "In the name of all travelers, hide us!"

Without a question, the man stood up and lifted the lid of the large wooden trunk on which he'd been sitting. "In," he said. "We use it for the disappearing maiden trick. Won't do that for you, I fear, but it is roomy."

No sooner had the lid lowered over them and Clarence resumed his seat than Kevin and Gina heard voices yelling in the street outside. "Search everything! Bertram will have our heads on pikes if those two get away."

Crammed against Gina in the musty darkness, Kevin felt the gold-entwined jewel press into his palm. If only he knew how to work this thing, they could whisk themselves away right now. Then it really would seem like a trick trunk. But he hadn't a clue. For all he knew, he had to click his heels together like Dorothy in Oz and whisper, "There's no place like home."

The thought filled him with pictures of home. He could see his mom and dad dressing up in their costumes and excitedly getting ready for the faire. Sure, it was phony and a little hokey, but right now he'd give anything to be there. To see the happy, picture-taking tourists, to see the bright, clean-smelling booths, to see Despard the Despicable charging along on his black steed wielding his sword against a honeydew with the same vigor as if it were an enemy skull . . .

The voices outside were closer now—almost upon

them. They were arguing with Clarence. Fiercely Kevin shut out that sound. He clutched Gina's hand and tried to think only of the world he wished he could see.

Roughly the lid was jerked up, and sunlight flooded in.

9

Program Change

In a dizzying blast of sunlight, the two children were thrown onto the ground. They tumbled and tumbled and landed not on the village street but on trampled grass. Horses' hooves pounded toward them. A sword flashed in the sun, and the innards of a honeydew melon splattered through the air.

As the crowd dutifully gasped and booed, Kevin and Gina staggered to their feet and gazed after the knight in red and black.

"Sir Despard!" they both yelled. "Despard of Norwood!"

At that last name, the knight turned. He raised the visor of his helmet, and his dark, bearded face glowered out.

"Despard, quick," Kevin yelled. "Bertram has found the medallion. He's going to marry Elfrieda!"

"We have come to take you back!" Gina added.

Slowly the knight turned his horse toward the two children. One of the faire organizers started stomping toward them to get the program back in order, but Despard angrily slashed his sword at him, and the official stopped short.

"All right," the knight growled, leaning down from his horse. "How do you know all this?"

"We've been there," Kevin said, holding up the blue jewel still clutched in his hand. "This is part of the magic that Bertram used to send you here."

Gina joined in. "And the jewel sent us back there. We talked to Elfrieda. She still wants to marry you but thought you were dead. She sent us to Norwood to find the jewel before Sir Bertram could, but he snatched it from us and now she has to marry him. Unless you go back and stop him."

"Then why dally?" Despard said gruffly, reaching for the jewel.

Just then the air shuddered with a silent explosion. People in the crowd gasped, then stumbled aside as a new knight made his way toward the lists. A huge knight on a huge brown horse, both splendid in armor and in green-and-brown livery.

"Brian the Beastly," Kevin and Gina whispered.

Scowling toward the newcomer, Sir Despard muttered, "Well, well, if it isn't my dear cousin's toady."

The faire's master of ceremonies was hopping about like a frustrated flea trying to question the new entrant. The massive knight ignored him. Raising his visor, he boomed out, "I have been sent by my master, Lord Bertram of Norwood, to challenge his cowardly runaway cousin to personal combat. Do you accept, Sir Despard?''

"I do!" the black-and-red knight shouted back. "And may you and your sniveling master rot in hell for what you have done to me and mine."

"No, wait!" Kevin yelled. "Despard, we don't have time for this. We need to go back!''

But the black knight ignored him, just as he did the confused crowd and the hair-tearing officials. Trotting his horse to one end of the lists, he lowered his lance. The green knight did the same at the other end, only his lance, unlike Despard's blunt-ended exhibition type, glinted with a wicked steel blade. For a moment the children stared in horror; then they scurried to get out of the way.

With a shout, Sir Brian gouged spurs into his horse's flanks, and the great animal plunged forward. Despard and his steed, which Kevin had thought so huge, now seemed dwarfed, but like a single furious beast they now burst into action, galloping down the field toward their opponent.

Armor flashed, hooves thudded. They drew nearer and nearer, then met. Despard's lance slipped past the green shield and smacked into Brian's armored chest. The shaft splintered and broke. The green knight swayed in his saddle but stayed put, as his own lance sliced through Despard's shield with such force that it ripped the shield from the black knight's arm.

Despard, too, kept in the saddle, but he was now

missing both lance and shield. Brian turned his horse and came again at his opponent. Hopelessly Despard pulled out his sword.

Kevin couldn't stand it. He ran forward, yelling, "Forget that guy, Despard! If you let him kill you, Bertram will keep your castle and your girl. That's where your fight is, not here!"

Seeming to ignore them again, Despard bore down on his adversary. At the last moment, horse and man sidestepped Brian's lance as Despard brought his sword down on the green shield, hacking off a corner. Then, with the green and brown knight still lumbering in the other direction, Despard swerved toward the children. Sheathing his sword, he leaned down and swung Kevin onto the rump of his horse and Gina up front against the arched neck.

Frantically Kevin clung to the knight's waist as the stallion plunged forward again.

"All right," Despard said, "we will go back. How is it done?"

"I don't know exactly," Kevin called. "Just get us away from here and give me a chance to work it out."

The black steed charged out the farm gate and down the road. Kevin turned and looked back. The green knight was following.

After several long blocks, the farm road ran into the highway. Without a pause Despard turned right, and they began galloping down the four-lane road.

Fearfully Kevin looked back again. If anything, the

green knight was gaining. His horse didn't have the burden of two extra passengers. Kevin would have thought a horse fresh from the Middle Ages would be scared of highway traffic, but the blinkered armor, he realized, must shut out most of that.

Kevin wished he had the same. He tried to shut out the sight of cars speeding along beside them with their curious pointing passengers. Sure, he wanted to yell, around here we always have knights in armor chasing each other down the highway. Instead he tried to concentrate on the jewel, on how it had worked before. He thought he had an inkling.

When he and Gina had first gone back, she had been describing her world so vividly, he'd been able to imagine it. And when they had returned here, he'd been trying to imagine his own world so he wouldn't have to face the world where he was about to get caught and maybe killed.

So, that could be it, he thought. Maybe that cracked old guy playing the hermit had been right. Imagination was the key.

"Hurry it up, boy," Despard yelled over the roar of cars and the clop of horses' hooves on pavement. "Sir Brian's lance is perilously close."

"I'm working on it!" Desperately Kevin tried to imagine the other jousting field, the medieval one. The smelly, noisy, excited crowd. The wind rippling banners. The willows and alders and ash trees, running like a rustling green wall between the sun-glinting river and the gold-and-white pavilion. Elfrieda with her red-gold hair and green gown, seated there, looking worried and stubborn. Beside her sat vile blond Bertram, looking smug.

A car horn honked. Kevin turned. Sir Brian's lance was within a few feet of skewering them like meat on a kabob.

10

Real Worlds

Kevin buried his face in Despard's surcoat, fighting fiercely to think of something besides cars and lances. Another surcoat. The same Norwood design on Bertram's trappings. The quartered black and red, and in its center a black boar's head blazoned on a red shield. Black and red gleaming in the bright English sun.

A car horn blared, then seemed to dwindle like a tortured siren. In its place rose the warbling notes of a trumpet.

Sun flashed in their eyes as they stumbled sickeningly to a halt. The white and gold of the Ashford Pavilion swayed before them. No, it was they who were swaying. Dizzily Kevin and Gina dismounted and let Despard walk his horse forward.

"Bertram," the knight called, raising his visor, "I charge you with foully using magic to send me from this world so that you might claim my castle, my lands, and my betrothed. I now reclaim my rights and challenge you to combat by the sword."

Slowly Bertram stood up, anger and hatred in his eyes. "So be it, cousin. This world was well rid of you once. I shall help it be so again."

Unsheathing his sword, he strode from the platform. Hurriedly an attendant handed him a shield as a knight in yellow and gray rode up to Despard and offered him his own shield.

Kevin and Gina scrambled onto the platform for a better view. Nobody objected or seemed to much notice. Glancing at Elfrieda, Kevin didn't blame her for looking worried. Despard might be bigger than Bertram, but he'd already had a tiring afternoon, and the "knights" he'd been practicing with this last year had not been the real thing. They'd been actors playing with imitation weapons.

The two knights lowered their visors and slowly began circling each other. Then Bertram lunged at his cousin, who took the sword thrust on his shield and launched an attack of his own. Again sword met shield. They began circling once more, looking for an opening. Despard lunged forward. Sword clashed against sword. The combatants stepped apart, then moved in again, their shields whacking together as each tried to throw the other off balance.

The battle went on and on with bone-jarring clash of shield, sword, and armor. With both wearing Norwood's red and black, it was sometimes hard to tell them apart, except for Despard's greater height and borrowed shield.

At last Bertram swung at his opponent with such force that the sword shied off the shield and sliced into the chain mail covering Despard's arm. Blood trickled between the metal links.

As the crowd groaned, Despard staggered and dropped to one knee. Bertram raised his sword, but the other brought his own blade flat against Bertram's knee, sending him stumbling backward. Despard rose to his feet then, hurled his shield away, grabbed his sword with both hands, and rained blows on his cousin's sword, shield, and body until Bertram toppled over and lay panting on the grass.

As Despard raised his sword again, Kevin had visions of a melon being replaced by a human head. But the black knight kept his sword upraised.

"I will not shed my own cousin's blood. Get you back to your lands in the north, Bertram. But if I ever see you in this part of England again, I will not be so forgiving. It is not for nothing that I have been called Despard the Despicable!"

Slowly Bertram rose to his feet, but as he turned to leave, Despard quickly reached forward and unfastened the jeweled belt from around his waist. "However this magic of yours works, I think it best not left in your care."

Bertram limped from the field accompanied by a few of his men, the rest seeming to feel that their true loyalty lay with Sir Despard. Elfrieda hiked up her green gown and hurried down the steps from the pavilion, followed by Gina and Kevin. Standing on tip-toes, the lady took off the medallion she was wearing and hung it around Despard's neck.

"There, now you can give it to me properly." Her smile turned questioning. "But how could anyone call you Despard the Despicable when you are such a sweetheart?"

"Oh, that is just a nickname I picked up. I have not been in the best of tempers lately. But I shall be from now on, my love."

Their kiss seemed so right that it was a moment before Kevin remembered to be embarrassed and look away.

By that time, Gina's family had pushed their way forward and were welcoming their daughter. Kevin, standing by himself, felt happy, tired, and just a little left out. But more than anything, he felt ready to go home.

A gauntleted hand clamped down on his shoulder. "From what I hear," Despard's deep voice said with a laugh, "I do not know if it is Kevin the Squire or Kevin the demon whom I should be thanking."

"Whichever fits," Kevin answered, noticing that when the knight smiled, he didn't look nearly as despicable.

"Well, in either case, you had better take these jewels of old Cuthbert's. They may have their uses, but they do not belong here."

Kevin took the offered belt. "No, and I guess I really don't either."

"Are you going home then?"

"If I can."

Suddenly Gina was beside him. "Are you sure you don't want to stay here, Kevin? This is the real thing, after all. You would not have to pretend anymore."

Kevin was hit with a surge of sadness but tried to turn it into a laugh. "Oh, I guess pretending isn't all bad. It's a lot safer, for one thing. Besides, it's real enough if that's what we really do in my world." He shook his head. "I do like it here, though. But, hey, it's . . . it's history. And I've got a life of my own to lead and a time of my own to do it in."

With a sudden excited smile, he added, "But, Gina, why don't you come back with me? There's a lot more to my time than mobile homes, TV, and Renaissance faires. Think of the adventure! I could show it all to you."

Gina smiled. "Yes, I guess you could find adventure in any time." Then she shook her head. "But, Kevin, that is your time and this is mine."

"But . . . but in my time you're *dead* already."

"So? To someone in the twenty-third century, so are you. But does that mean that your life is not worth living when you have it?" Grabbing Kevin's hands, she smiled impishly. "But I have to admit, Kevin the Squire, troublesome as you are, I will miss you. You are not such a bad fellow in either time."

She placed a quick, soft kiss on his cheek and then stepped back. "Now you had better be going before I start acting silly. Have you finally figured out how to work those things?"

Kevin tried to hide his pleased surprise in a businesslike answer. "Yes, I think so. But I agree with Despard; these jewels are a pack of trouble. I'll use them to go home, but I really wish they could go where they belong as well."

Knights and nobles were now crowding around, welcoming Sir Despard and congratulating him and his lady. Sun glinted off armor while a breeze from the river fluttered at the boldly colored surcoats and the veils and sleeves trailing from the ladies' gowns. From the wider crowd of merchants, peasants, and travelers came the festive sounds of talking and laughter and someone singing a ballad only slightly off-key. Clarence the actor pushed through the crowd and swept Gina off her feet in a welcoming hug. She laughed joyously, and her dark hair bobbed about in a carefree cascade.

With a pang, Kevin watched it all. It was all so medieval, so very real; how could he possibly leave? And yet, real or not, it wasn't where he *really* belonged.

Clutching the jewels, he closed his eyes and tried to imagine the place and time where he did belong: the Sixth Annual Southern Indiana Renaissance Faire as it had been the day he left it. There'd be nylon tents, playacting participants in too-clean costumes, and gawking, camera-toting tourists. The crowd would smell of little besides deodorant, and mingling with the sound of talking and laughter would be lilting madrigals a little too well sung, while in the distance there'd be the faint rumble of highway traffic.

After a moment's wrenching dizziness, Kevin opened his eyes on the green Indiana countryside with water tower and power lines rising beyond the trees. Behind him, he could hear the happy sounds of the faire. So what if it was make-believe, he thought defiantly. People were *really* enjoying themselves, weren't they? And that is one kind of "real," isn't it?

Gratefully he spun around, then noticed that the jeweled belt was no longer in his hand. Well, maybe it had gone back to where it belonged as well. No great loss. He'd had about all the heroic adventure he could take for a while.

The next thing he noticed was that his digital watch was working again. He stared. It was showing the same day that he had left and only a couple of hours later, right after the last scheduled joust. That was the way he had tried to imagine it, and now here it was. Outstanding! Now he wouldn't have to explain nearly as much to his parents.

Looking around, he took a deep breath, trying to drink in the whole scene. With a smile, he wondered how long it would take the jousting company to train their new designated villain, Brian the Beastly. Maybe the fellow would really take to this century. In his off hours he could work as a TV wrestler or a bouncer at a bar.

"So, my fine young squire, have you done any further growing up of late?"

Startled, Kevin turned to see the old crackpot who dressed up as a hermit. "Growing up? Oh, you mean about imagination and all. Well, yeah, maybe I have kind of grown into it again. I guess imagination does have its uses."

"Ha! Glad you have noticed, boy. I rather thought you had promise. Well, got to be hobbling off to my hermit cave. Lots of meditating to do, you know, and all that other stuff we quaint medieval hermits supposedly engage in."

As the old man started to shuffle off, Kevin noticed the belt of blue jewels around his waist.

"Cuthbert! You're old Cuthbert!"

"The same. A sweet girl, that Elfrieda. I do hope she will be very happy with her knight in that drafty old castle of hers."

"But aren't you going to use the jewels to go back now?"

"Not on your life, boy! That Bertram was an unimaginative half-wit. He never figured out how to tune the jewels to anything other than the time and place where I happened to have them set on the day he snatched them. Sure, I'll be using them—but go back to the Middle Ages? No way! Think about it. No pizza, no TV, fleas in the beds, and people dying of plague. No, thank you!''

The old man leaned forward. Under his bushy gray eyebrows, his eyes flashed a lively blue. ''Hey, it took this century to show me exactly what imagination can do. The possibilities are endless, kid!''

''But where will you go?''

''Well, you know, I've gotten pretty good at imagining a twenty-fourth century starship.'' With a jaunty wave, he turned away. ''Have a good life, kid.''

Kevin watched until the old man disappeared into the crowd. Only then did he remember the last jewel. Quickly he reached into his pouch. The video game and coins were long gone, but his fingers touched and brought out something else. The twining gold work and faceted jewel sparkled in the sun. Well, maybe he'd keep it—just as a souvenir.

Still, he thought as he tucked the jewel away, like old Cuthbert said, when it comes to imagination, the possibilities are endless.

Whistling the little Gypsy tune about the freed bird, Kevin walked back toward the faire.

ENTER THE WORLD OF
PAMELA SERVICE

BEING OF TWO MINDS
Connie Hendricks is a typical American teen who has spells that make her pass out. When this happens, Connie enters the mind and soul of Prince Rudolph, a fourteen-year-old heir apparent of Thulgaria, a small European country. Everything is just fine—until Rudolph is kidnapped while Connie is inside his mind.

THE RELUCTANT GOD
Lorna Padgett takes a walk in the Egyptian hills near her father's archeological dig and meets Ameni, a young man who will turn her world upside down. Ameni is not a typical teen. He is the son of a pharaoh who lived four thousand years ago, and he draws Lorna into an adventure across time and space.

STINKER FROM SPACE
In the middle of an outer space battle, space warrior Tsynq Yr crash-lands on earth and is forced to enter the body of a skunk. This space-age skunk must get home with top-secret information to ensure his planet's victory. Luckily, he runs into Karen and her computer-whiz friend, who hatch a crazy scheme to get this skunk back into orbit.

UNDER ALIEN STARS
Jason Sikes cannot believe his mother willingly works side by side with the Tsorians, an alien race that conquered the Earth. Aryl, the daughter of a Tsorian commander, finds Earthlings uncouth and primitive. Jason and Aryl are sworn enemies until they must join together to fight an even more deadly evil.

VISION QUEST
His name is Wadat and he is an ancient Indian shaman who travels across time to find peace. Kate Elliot has lost her father, and she and her mother are trying to start over in a half-deserted mining town. Kate is lonely and miserable until she finds a small, smooth stone that unleashes an ancient Indian secret and its mysterious and healing magic.

WHEN THE NIGHT WIND HOWLS
New to town, Sidonie Guthrie joins a local theater group to meet people...not ghosts! Sid decides to spend the night at the haunted, old theater to confront the ghostly apparitions that walk the stage, and she is treated to the performance of a lifetime.

Look for these books by
PAMELA SERVICE
in your local bookstore.

Published by Fawcett Books.